Danny and the BLUE CLOUD

Coping With Childhood Depression

by James M. Foley, DEd
illustrated by Shirley Ng-Benitez

Magination Press • Washington, DC • American Psychological Association

For Beth, wife, mother, and teacher
who turned blue clouds into rainbows—*JMF*

With love and sincere gratitude
to my dear mom and dad—*SN-B*

Published by
MAGINATION PRESS®
An Educational Publishing Foundation Book
American Psychological Association
750 First Street NE
Washington, DC 20002

Magination Press is a registered trademark of the American Psychological Association.

For more information about our books, including a complete catalog, please write to us, call
1-800-374-2721, or visit our website at www.apa.org/pubs/magination.

Book design by Gwen Grafft
Printed by Lake Book Manufacturing, Inc., Melrose Park, IL

Library of Congress Cataloging-in-Publication Data

Names: Foley, James M., 1947– | Ng-Benitez, Shirley, illustrator.
Title: Danny and the blue cloud : coping with childhood depression /
  by James M. Foley, DEd ; illustrated by Shirley Ng-Benitez.
Description: Washington, DC : Magination Press, [2016] | "American
  Psychological Association." | Summary: "Danny the bear has a blue cloud
  of depression hanging over his head; he gets help with his blue cloud from
  Barnaby the rabbit"— Provided by publisher.
Identifiers: LCCN 2015014375 | ISBN 9781433821035 (hardcover) |
  ISBN 1433821036 (hardcover)
Subjects: | CYAC: Depression, Mental—Fiction. | Bears—Fiction. |
  Rabbits—Fiction. | Forest animals—Fiction.
Classification: LCC PZ7.1.F65 Dan 2016 | DDC [E]—dc23 LC record
  available at http://lccn.loc.gov/2015014375

Manufactured in the United States of America
First printing December 2015
10 9 8 7 6 5 4 3 2 1

Danny was born
under a blue cloud.

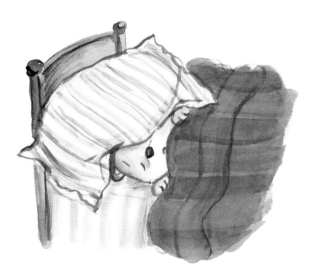

He didn't know why,
but sometimes the
cloud made him cry.

Some days the cloud seemed as big
as the whole sky. On those days,
Danny didn't want to get out of bed
and moved as slowly as the turtles.

Some days,
Danny was
one big GROWL!

The other animals came
to Danny's house to ask
him to come out and play,
but Danny's cloud felt
heavy and dark.

After a while, Danny didn't even
go to the door when his friends came.
He stayed in his room.

Danny thought, "I never run and climb
and play. I must be the worst runner,
climber, and player in the forest."

When the Grand Forest Parade happened, he didn't go outside to watch.
His mother said, "That's all right, Danny, it's okay to stay inside."

One day, while Danny was sitting in his room, *Wham! Bam! Bebop! Wham Bam Bebop!* He opened the window just as Barnaby the rabbit landed on two huge feet!

"By Uncle Wally's whiskers, what are you doing inside
on a nice day like today?" Barnaby said.
"This is hopping, climbing, and playing weather!"

"I have never played in the forest. Besides, I am the worst
runner, climber, and player in the forest," Danny said.

"If you have never climbed or played in
the forest, how do you know that you are the
worst climber and player in the forest?
Come on outside, we need to talk.

Danny boy, you need to be DEFUNKIFIED!"

"Ummm … Barnaby, what does defunkified mean?"

"YOU NEED TO FEEL BETTER!

Did you know that if you change the way you think,
you can change the way you feel?

It sounds like you are thinking about all of the bad
things and not the good things that are possible.

Let's make a list of all the things that you can do!
Okay, Danny Boy, NUMBER ONE!"

Danny mumbled to himself and hopped once on one paw and then once on the other. "I cannn.....ah..."

Danny hopped twice on one paw and then twice on the other. "I ahhh..."

Danny hopped three times on one paw and then three times on the other.

"STOP!" said Barnaby. "While you were trying to think, you were DOING some first-class hopping. As a rabbit, I am an expert judge of hopping, and if you can hop then you can dance. Let me see you hop again."

Barnaby started to whistle a happy tune
and clap along. All of a sudden, Danny felt
his body start to move to the music.

His arms and legs seemed to move
all by themselves.

Danny could hear the music
in his head and felt like he was
floating across the forest floor.

"WHY SHUT MY MOUTH AND CALL ME A CARROT! Danny, you are not just a dancer, you are a BOOGIE MACHINE." Danny smiled.

"Danny, did you notice how you didn't feel like dancing until you started dancing?

Remember that tune. Hear the tune in your head and start dancing even if you don't feel like it.

Think 'I am a great dancer. And I feel better whenever I move my body.' Thinking good thoughts about yourself is another trick to feel better. Good thoughts make good feelings!"

"Danny, remember these FEEL-GOOD RULES."

BARNABY'S FEEL-GOOD RULES

- Think about GOOD things instead of focusing on just the BAD things.

- Think about what you CAN do and not what you CAN'T do.

- Dance even when you don't want to dance. MOVING MAKES YOU FEEL BETTER!

- Think GOOD things about yourself, even if it feels easier to think bad things.

Danny danced and danced. He danced
even when his cloud felt heavy.
The more he danced, the better he felt.

Soon, the animals noticed Danny
dancing and wanted to learn.

Danny taught Barnaby's
bunny buddies to dance.

He taught the raccoons,
the weasels, and even the turtles.

When Danny's blue cloud started to feel heavy and dark, he practiced Barnaby's Feel-Good Rules.

He thought about what he CAN do, and not what he CAN'T DO.

He thought about GOOD things instead of focusing on just the BAD things.

He danced, even when he didn't feel like it.

He thought GOOD things
about himself.

The blue cloud was beginning to change color.
It became lighter and brighter.

The more Danny danced and taught the other
animals to dance, the brighter his cloud became.

The Grand Forest Parade and Celebration would soon be happening. One day the wise old owl and leader of the forest called all the animals together.

The owl said, "This year's Grand Forest Parade will be the biggest and best ever.

It will be the most joyful because we will all dance.

For all his hard work, I am naming Danny
the Bear as the Official Forest Dance Instructor
and Grand Marshal of the Forest Parade."

All the animals cheered and raised
Danny up on their shoulders.

Just then Barnaby shouted,
"Danny, look up over your head!"

Danny looked up and smiled.
His cloud was shining with all
the colors of the rainbow.

Danny smiled because he had learned Barnaby's
Feel-Good Rules. He knew that he had the power to
change the biggest, bluest cloud into a beautiful rainbow!

Note to Parents and Caregivers

Depression is often thought of as a condition that affects adults, but in fact, children can experience depression as well. As a parent, it is a difficult task to recognize and deal with depression in a young child. However, the good news is that childhood depression is highly treatable and early intervention is the key to success. You may have struggled with your own clinical depression, or a history of depression may exist in your extended family, but it is important to realize that depression is not caused by a failure in parenting. Childhood depression is the result of a complex mix of neurological factors and life circumstances.

Depression is not the same thing as a passing bad mood or sadness. When your child is experiencing passing sadness or stress, your soothing and reassurances may be enough to improve your child's mood. When your attempts at comforting do not reduce the intensity and frequency of your child's sadness, anxiety, or anger over time, childhood depression may be present.

Significant signs of childhood depression include:

- Displays of anger, opposition, or withdrawal, such as frequent tantrums, that are out of character for your child and not part of his or her normal development
- Changes in appetite and sleep routine
- Increase in negative self-statements (such as "I'm a dummy," or "I'll never be able to do this!")
- Increased crying
- Lack of interest in activities previously enjoyed
- Talking or focusing on death
- Thoughts of self-harm or suicidal plans

Remember, early intervention is the key to successful treatment. If you have not already contacted a qualified professional, it is recommended that you pursue at least an initial screening session. Speaking to your child's school counselor, school administration, or pediatrician is a good place to start for a referral. If your child has suicidal thoughts or plans, seek help immediately.

HOW THIS BOOK CAN HELP

Danny and the Blue Cloud addresses the subject of childhood depression through the actions of Danny and his forest friends. Danny exhibits symptoms of childhood depression: he cries, withdraws from friends, and loses interest in playing. However, with the help of Barnaby the bunny, Danny learns to reshape his thinking in a more helpful fashion.

The bedtime story often presents a precious opportunity for children to share their inner world and perceptions with their parents. Reading *Danny and the Blue Cloud* can help spark such conversations with your child. As you read the story with your child, try asking questions such as "How do you think Danny feels?" "Do you ever feel that way?" and "What did Danny do to feel better?" Hopefully, discussions of the story will foster your child's emotional growth and strengthen the bond between you and your child.

COGNITIVE-BEHAVIORAL THERAPY

The strategies used in the story to help Danny cope with his depression are examples of cognitive-behavioral therapy interventions. Depression is often characterized by distorted thinking that leads to a pattern of unhelpful behavior and feelings. Research has supported that a change in thinking can lead to a change in behavior and feelings.

By presenting and implementing a series of "Feel-Good Rules," Barnaby helped Danny change his thinking and then his behavior into a more helpful pattern. The result was a happier mood!

Think about GOOD things instead of focusing on just the BAD things. Depressed children often view life through a distorted lens and view only the negative aspects. They tend to be rigid or "black and white" in their thinking. By asking Danny to think of good things in addition to the bad, Barnaby challenges Danny's black-and-white thinking.

Think about what you CAN do and not what you CAN'T do. By focusing on his skills and abilities, Danny develops mastery and a pattern of optimism.

Dance even when you don't want to dance. MOVING MAKES YOU FEEL BETTER! Lethargy or lack of energy is often the result of depression. Physical movement activates the "feel-good" chemical agents in the brain.

Think GOOD things about yourself, even if it feels easier to think bad things. "Self-talk," or the words we say to ourselves, can affect our mood. By changing his unhelpful self-talk into helpful self-talk, Danny increases his self-esteem.

You may wish to review the strategies presented in the book with your child's therapist to learn more. In addition to these strategies, there are ways that you can connect with your child and support his or her treatment at home.

HOW TO SUPPORT YOUR CHILD'S TREATMENT

Meeting with a licensed mental health professional is the first and most important step in treating childhood depression. Here are a few basic ideas for assisting your child's treatment. These strategies can be helpful in the healthy development of all children.

Communicate. Establish regular rituals that provide the opportunity for an open dialogue with your child. For example, you may read a story to your child at bedtime, when your child is comfortable in his or her own bed surrounded by familiar stuffed animals. However, you can also have regular talks with your child in the car or at the dinner table. No matter when or where your communication takes place, give your child your full attention.

Listen first. Listening is a sign of caring and respect. It also provides you with a view of the world through your child's eyes. Your understanding of events may be very different from your child's perception. Listening helps you determine if your child views a situation as problematic. In discussions with your child, use open-ended questions that address broad topics ("Tell me about your day at preschool.") Follow up on your child's answers ("Sounds like it was not such a good day?") to clarify your child's point of view. Try to keep your responses neutral, such as "I see how you feel," or "It's hard to feel that way." By keeping your statements neutral, you empathize with your child and help him or her feel understood, without appearing judgmental.

Be patient. If your child does not answer a question during a discussion, it does not mean that your child is not listening. Your instinct as a parent may be to ask more questions in order to gain more information. Try to wait and let your child respond when he or she is comfortable. Try not to take it personally if your child does not want to talk; remind your child that you are there for

him or her when your child does feel like talking. Your patience will be paid off by gathering valid information delivered at a time of your child's choosing.

Observe your child's patterns of behavior. As a parent, you know your child's regular emotional and behavioral patterns. Be aware of the signs and symptoms of depression, and pay attention to radical shifts in your child's pattern of emotional and behavioral expression. Discuss changes with your child's therapist.

Encourage your child's problem-solving behavior. Positive self-esteem is built on a foundation of competent problem solving. Let your child attempt to solve problem situations before giving your solutions. Find a balance between emotionally supporting your child and empowering your child to face adversity. When your child is facing a problem (such as resolving a conflict with siblings or peers), you might try asking questions such as "What could you do to make things better?" and "What would happen then?" Support your child's problem-solving with statements such as, "That's a good idea," and "You could do that and also …" Fostering successful problem solving leads to a pattern of life-long optimism. When your child faces problems and perseveres, he or she builds the resiliency necessary to cope with future issues.

Move. Physical activity is an important component of mental health. Pick a physical activity that your child enjoys. Engage in the activity with your child on a regular schedule, especially if your child appears "down."

Remember to take care of yourself! Barnaby's "Feel-Good Rules" are not just for your child, they apply to you also. You can support your child's treatment by ensuring you feel your best as well. If you notice symptoms of anxiety and depression in yourself, or if you have a past pattern of difficulty occurring in your personal life, seek help from a licensed mental health professional.

Reading this book is not a substitute for therapy. If you notice signs or symptoms of depression in your child, it is recommended that you seek help from a licensed mental health professional. Seek help immediately if your child has suicidal thoughts or plans for self-harm. With early intervention, depression is treatable. However, it is important to continue to monitor your child's emotional and behavioral patterns for signs and symptoms of depression as he or she gets older.

About the Author

James M. Foley, DEd, is a licensed psychologist who has recently retired from his private practice in Maine. He has served as a clinical director and member of a community mental health center children's service team and has extensive experience as a school psychologist and child and family therapist. He now resides in Sonoma County, CA, in close proximity to his two adult children, and serves as psychological consultant to a local school district.

About the Illustrator

Shirley Ng-Benitez loves to draw! She is a graduate of San Jose State University, with a bachelor's in graphic design and a concentration in illustration. Since '98, she's owned gabbyandco.com, a design, illustration, and handlettering firm. She's inspired by her family, nature, food, travel, and music—especially the guitar, ukulele, piano, and violin music played by her husband and daughters daily. She creates with watercolor, gouache, pencil, and digital techniques and is living her dream, illustrating and writing picture books in San Martin, CA. You can find more of her work on her website, www.shirleyngbenitez.com.

About Magination Press

Magination Press is an imprint of the American Psychological Association, the largest scientific and professional organization representing psychologists in the United States and the largest association of psychologists worldwide.